Hansel and Gretel
and
The Princess and the Pea

Retold by Rose Impey
Illustrated by Peter Bailey

ORCHARD BOOKS

Hansel and Gretel

Once upon a time, on the edge of a deep wood, there lived a poor woodcutter. He had a wife and two children – a boy called Hansel and a girl called Gretel. The wife wasn't the children's real mother, who had died when they were still young. No, the man had married a second time and he often had cause to regret it.

Being poor, the family usually had little to eat, but when there came a hard winter they had even less.

One night the man lay awake in bed, too worried to sleep.

"Oh, Wife," he said, "what's going to become of us? We haven't enough food to last the week. Then what will we do?"

"I know exactly what we'll do. We'll take the children into the woods and leave them there. If we're lucky they won't find their way back. Then at least *we* may survive."

"I couldn't think of it," said the man. "Even if they didn't starve to death, wild animals would get them."

"Then we'll all starve," said his wife. "Take your pick, it's either them or us."

The man hated his wife's idea, but he couldn't come up with a better one. Finally she talked him round, which was a way she had, and the man went to sleep with a heavy heart.

But the children were also lying awake. They'd overheard their parents, and now Gretel lay beside her brother crying.

"Oh, Hansel, what are we going to do?" she sobbed.

"Don't cry, Gretel. I won't let anything happen to you."

Hansel got out of bed, put on his clothes and crept outside. The moon was full and shone down, picking out hundreds of white pebbles that glittered like new coins. Hansel collected as many as he could fit into his pockets. Then he crept back to bed.

Early next morning their stepmother woke them roughly.

"Get up, you slugabeds. We're going to the woods. Dress yourselves quickly. Your father and I can't wait all day."

Before they set off she gave them each a crust of bread.

"This is all you'll be getting today, you'd better make it last."

Hansel gave his piece to Gretel, to carry in her apron. His own pockets were full of stones.

As they walked along the path into the woods, Hansel kept stopping and turning back.

"Look lively, son," said his father, "you're facing the wrong way."

But Hansel said, "I was just watching the cat, Father. It's sitting on the roof, waving to me."

"Don't be an idiot," snapped his stepmother. "That's not a cat, it's simply the sun shining on the chimney."

But Hansel wasn't really looking back to see the cat. He was stopping, from time to time, to drop a pebble on the path.

When they were deep into the woods their parents sent the children to collect firewood. Then their father made them a good fire.

"Now, you two sit there and don't wander off," said their stepmother. "Later you can eat your bread and have a rest. We're going to do our work. We shan't be far away. We'll come back for you before it gets dark."

So the children did as they were told and rested and ate their food. They saw

no reason to worry, because quite close by they could hear the sound of an axe on wood. Or they thought they could. But it was really a loose branch their parents had carefully tied to a tree so that it knocked against it in the wind. That's what they could hear.

At last, from hunger and boredom, the children fell asleep. When they woke it was getting dark and Gretel was afraid.

"How will we ever find our way home?" she said.

"Don't worry," said Hansel, "Wait till the moon comes up, then we'll have no trouble."

Sure enough, when the moon shone down on the pebbles, they stood out clearly, marking a trail that led them all the way home.

It was nearly dawn by the time they reached their house. The children knocked at the door to be let in. When their stepmother saw them standing there, she was furious.

"Fancy staying out all night, you scoundrels. Worrying your father and me like that! We thought you were never coming home."

But now their father could stop worrying. He felt as if a stone had been lifted from his heart. And, for a while, life was kind to them all and they survived.

However, it's usually true that 'once poor, always poor'. Before long the family were once again close to starvation.

"Well that's the last loaf. When that's gone the crying'll really start," said the man's wife. "This time we must take those children so deep into the woods they'll never find their way out."

Their father had been dreading this. He thought they should all stick together – even if they had to starve. But he'd given in to his wife once and the second time was no different. The man was a coward, and cowards can be cruel too.

Again the children had lain awake and overheard what was said. When their parents were asleep, Hansel got up and tried to go out. But this time his stepmother had locked and bolted the door and he had to creep back to bed. Again he comforted his little sister. "Don't worry, Gretel. Everything'll be all right. I'll look after you."

The next morning, before the sun rose, their stepmother got out of bed. She gave them each a small piece of bread and soon they set off along the path, Hansel, as last time, lagging behind.

"Shake a leg, lad," said his father. "You'll meet yourself coming back, if you're not careful."

"I was just watching the dove, Father. It's sitting on the roof, waving to me."

 "Fool," said his stepmother. "That's not a dove, it's simply the sun shining on the chimney." But Hansel wasn't really looking back at the dove. He was stopping, from time to time, to crumble the bread in his pocket and scatter the crumbs along the path.

This time, their parents took Hansel and Gretel far deeper into the woods than last time, further than they'd ever been before. Again their father built a fire and told them to rest and wait till evening when he would come back for them.

At noon the children ate their food. They shared Gretel's piece of bread, because Hansel had crumbled his on the path. Again they fell asleep and only woke when it was already dark. Gretel was afraid, but Hansel assured her that once the moon was up they'd soon find their way home.

However, when the moon rose, there wasn't a single crumb to be seen. Birds had flown down and eaten every one the moment it was dropped. This time there was no trail to follow.

"Don't worry, Gretel," said Hansel. "We'll find our way."

But they didn't. The children walked and walked, through the night and all the next day, hoping they would come to a place they recognised, but they only wandered even deeper into the woods. Tall trees packed tightly together cut out most of the sunshine, and the children walked all day in their shade. They felt cold and helpless. All they could find to eat were a few nuts and berries. At last they were so tired that they fell asleep huddled together beneath a bush.

On the third morning they were still lost, and began to think they might starve to death in that dreadful place.

Suddenly their attention was drawn towards a pure white bird, which perched in the branches above them singing sweetly. When it flew off they began to follow it. The bird came to rest on the roof of a house, in the middle of a clearing. And what a strange house it was.

From a distance it *looked* good enough to eat. When they came closer they found it *was*.

The house was made entirely out of gingerbread and cake, and the windows were made of barley sugar. Hansel reached up and took a piece off the roof, and Gretel licked the window pane. The children fell on the house greedily.

Suddenly a voice came from inside.
"Nibble, nibble, little mouse,
Who's that nibbling at my house?"

The children didn't stop eating for a moment. They called back,

"It's only two birds having a rest,
Borrowing crumbs to build their nest."

Soon both children were gobbling the wall, breaking off huge chunks of cake. They were holding a piece in each hand when the door of the house opened and out came the ugliest old woman you ever saw. Hansel and Gretel were so scared they dropped what they were eating and stood like a pair of statues.

But to their surprise, the old woman spoke kindly to them.

"Why, what sweet little children! Wherever did you come from? Don't be afraid; come inside and sit down. No one's going to eat you."

And she took them by the hand and drew them into the house. She fed them up with pancakes and honey and milk and baked apples until they couldn't eat another bite. And then she led them upstairs and tucked them into two soft little beds with pure white quilts. The children lay there and thought they must be in heaven.

But they were not – far from it. They were in the hands of a wicked witch who was always in wait for any children who might come her way. She'd made this gingerbread house specially to tempt them in. Once she'd got them inside, she would fatten them up and eat them. Children were her favourite delicacy.

As soon as Hansel and Gretel had come nearby she had smelled them. Witches have a powerful sense of smell, just like animals. This is to make up for their eyes, which are often red, and almost useless. They can hardly see at all.

So the next morning when the witch crept up the stairs on her hard little feet, she had to bend right down low over the children. Only then could she see their round red cheeks. Mmmmm, they made her mouth water.

"These'll make a tasty meal," she said to herself. She grabbed Hansel with her horrible horny hand, dragged him out of bed and pulled him down the stairs. She took him outside and locked him in a wooden cage.

It made no difference to her how he struggled and screamed; witches have no hearts. Then she went back upstairs and roughly shook Gretel too.

"Get up, you lazy lump. Go and get the water and put it to boil. We must cook something special for your brother to fatten him up. Then, when he's a nice rolypoly pudding, I'm going to eat him."

Gretel burst out crying, such terrible tears, but tears were wasted on the witch. In the end Gretel was made to do as she was told.

From now on Hansel had the very best of food, while poor Gretel had little more than a crab's claw to chew on. Each day the witch went out to check how Hansel was doing.

"Hansel, put out your finger. I want to see if you're fat enough yet."

But instead Hansel poked out a chicken bone and the witch, who couldn't see further than her nose, thought it was his finger. She couldn't understand how, with so much to eat, the boy seemed to get no fatter.

After four weeks her patience ran out. She wouldn't wait any longer.

"Well, ready or not, tomorrow we shall chop him up and boil him in a stew."

Then poor Gretel cried. She sobbed and she pleaded. She prayed for help. But the witch told her to save her breath.

"Stop your bawling, child, it'll do you no good."

The next day, when Gretel got up, she was ordered to fill the cauldron and hang it over the fire to get the water ready.

"But first we'll do some baking," said the witch. "I've made the dough. You, dear child, can help me by testing the oven. Creep in, there's a good girl, and check it's hot enough."

And she pushed Gretel to the oven door. Great flames were already pouring out of it. Gretel was no fool; she knew what the witch intended. She would push Gretel inside and bake her; then she would eat her too.

So Gretel said, "I don't know how to tell. And I don't think I could fit in there."

"You stupid child," snapped the witch, pushing Gretel aside. "Have you no brains? Even I could fit in. Look, like this."

And the witch stuck her own head inside the oven door. Then Gretel came

up behind her. With an almighty
push she tumbled the witch inside.
She slammed the iron door shut and
fastened the bolt.

Oh! You should have heard that
witch howl! But Gretel didn't wait to
listen. She ran off and left her to be
baked to a crisp. She ran straight out to
Hansel and unlocked his cage.

"Hansel, we're free," she cried out.
"The old witch is dead."

Hansel sprang out of the cage and the two of them hugged each other and danced around the yard. The witch was gone, and now there was nothing to be afraid of. The two children went back into the house, and were amazed to find trunks full of pearls and jewels.

Hansel filled his pockets with them. "These are more useful than pebbles," he said. And Gretel too filled her apron until it was overflowing.

30

"Now, we need to get out of these dreadful woods and find our way home," said Hansel.

They walked for several hours until they came to a lake which stretched before them, blocking their way.

"How can we possibly get across?" said Hansel. "There isn't a bridge or a boat."

"Look," said Gretel. "Over there's a white swan." And she called out and asked the swan to carry them across the water.

The swan came closer and Hansel climbed on her back. "Come on, Gretel," he said.

But Gretel refused, thinking it would be too much for the swan.

"Let her take us one at a time," she said.

So that's what the swan did. Once they were both safely across they went on, hoping they would find their way home. Gradually they came to places they recognised and at last they spotted the chimney of their father's house.

Then, tired as they were, they began to run. They burst through the door and threw themselves upon their father's neck. The poor man thought he must be dreaming, or gone mad. Since he had left his children in the woods he hadn't known a moment's peace. His wife had left him. She'd been unable to bear his misery at the loss of the children, so that had been some compensation. But all he wanted now was to have his children back.

Gretel emptied her apron of jewels into her father's lap until they spilled on to the kitchen floor and Hansel added his too. Now they need never be poor again. Their worries were at an end, and the three of them could live together in peace and happiness at last.

The Princess and the Pea

Once upon a time there was a
prince who wanted to marry, so
what did he do? He looked for a
princess, of course. But she had to be a
real princess. Nothing else would do.
He travelled all over the world to find
one, but without success.

There were plenty to choose from,
at least, plenty who *said* they were real

princesses. But the prince
could never be sure.

There were no end
of beautiful girls who
put the sun to shame.
There were any number
of girls who could sing as
sweetly as a bird
and a dozen who could
dance and wear out
a pair of slippers
in an evening.
There were
countless girls
who were immensely
rich and even more
who had *been* rich, but
now were terribly poor.

There was no shortage of girls who had ugly sisters and cruel stepmothers. There were one or two girls who told him they'd been locked up in towers, and one who claimed she'd been to sleep for a hundred years! There was even a girl who said she'd once kissed a frog. But no matter what they told him, the prince never knew whether to believe them. He could never be *absolutely* sure.

Finally the prince returned home, sad and disappointed, because he had so set his heart on finding a real princess.

His mother, the queen, hated to see her son so despondent.

"Don't worry, my dear. When the right girl comes along, I shall know how to tell. You leave it entirely to me."

One night there was a terrible storm in the city. The heavens opened and the rain fell in sheets like a waterfall. There was thunder and lightning. Something had upset the weather and now it was taking out its temper on the world.

Suddenly there was a
loud knocking at the
city gates and the king
himself went to see
who was there.
When he opened the
gates he saw a most
forlorn and pathetic
figure, who said she
was a princess.

She was soaked to the
skin. Her hair was dripping
wet and hung like rats' tails. Her
clothes were sticking to her, and even
her shoes were awash with water. To be
blunt about it, she looked a poor
bedraggled creature, but she *said* she
was a real princess.

And that was the truth, she was. She was presently on her travels around the world, in search of a prince. She was now old enough to marry and had set her heart on finding a *real* prince; nothing else would do. She had already met plenty who *said* they were real princes, but somehow she had a feeling they weren't.

There were no end of handsome young men who only had to be looked upon to be loved. There were any

number of brave young men who had
apparently slain dragons or demons or
devils – some said with their bare hands.
There were countless young men who
had been turned into beasts, or birds,
or frogs. There was even one young
man who said he had hacked his way
through a hedge, half a mile deep, to
rescue a princess.

But no matter what they told her, the
princess couldn't bring herself to believe
them. She could never be *absolutely* sure.

And so here she was, still on her travels, feeling sad and disappointed. She had *so* set her heart on finding a real prince.

When the royal family first saw her, dripping on the palace floors, they were not easily convinced either. How could they tell if she were a real princess, the state she was in? The poor prince was as confused as ever. But the queen knew exactly what to do. "Come with me," she told him. "We'll soon find out."

They went together
to the bedchamber,
where the princess
was to sleep. The
queen told the prince
to take the mattress
off the bed. Then
she laid a single
pea at the base of
the bed. On top
of it they laid
twenty mattresses.
And then, on top
of those, they laid
twenty feather beds.
And that was the
bed the princess
was to sleep in.

43

All through the night the princess lay awake. She tossed and turned. She wriggled and she jiggled in the bed to try to make herself more comfortable, but it was no use. By morning she was perfectly miserable.

When she came down for breakfast, the queen asked, "Did you sleep well, my dear?"

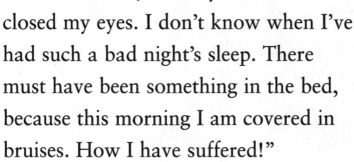

But the princess replied, "No, I'm afraid I didn't. In fact, I hardly closed my eyes. I don't know when I've had such a bad night's sleep. There must have been something in the bed, because this morning I am covered in bruises. How I have suffered!"

And then the prince *knew* that she must be a real princess. Who else could have felt a single pea through twenty mattresses and twenty feather beds? Only a real princess would be so sensitive.

"For years, I have been looking for a real princess," said the prince. "Now that I've found you, will you marry me?"

The princess considered this carefully. If he could know with such certainty that she was a *real* princess, which she was, then surely it must follow that he was indeed a *real* prince too. (And he was.)

Now, when a real and handsome prince meets a real and beautiful princess, it's only natural that he should ask her to marry him. And what could be more natural than for her to accept? So she did.

And what should they both do then? Why, live happily ever after, of course. And they did.

And so, I hope, will you.

HANS CHRISTIAN ANDERSEN TALES FROM ORCHARD BOOKS

RETOLD BY ANDREW MATTHEWS
ILLUSTRATED BY PETER BAILEY

☐ 1 **The Emperor's New Clothes and The Tinder Box**
   1 84121 663 1   £3.99
☐ 2 **The Little Matchgirl and The Wild Swans**
   1 84121 675 5   £3.99
☐ 3 **The Little Mermaid and The Princess and the Pea**
   1 84121 667 4   £3.99
☐ 4 **Thumbelina and The Tin Soldier**
   1 84121 671 2   £3.99

Orchard Fairy Tales are available from all good bookshops,
or can be ordered direct from the publisher:
Orchard Books, PO BOX 29, Douglas IM99 1BQ
Credit card orders please telephone 01624 836000
or fax 01624 837033
or e-mail: bookshop@enterprise.net for details.

To order please quote title, author and ISBN
and your full name and address.
Cheques and postal orders should be
made payable to 'Bookpost plc'.
Postage and packing is FREE within the UK
(overseas customers should add £1.00 per book).

Prices and availability are subject to change.